50

Happy Birthday Bugs

This Looney Tunes Library Book is published by Longmeadow Press
in association with Sammis Publishing.
Distributed by Book Sales, Inc., 110 Enterprise Ave.,
Secaucus, NJ 07904

With special thanks to
Guy Gilchrist • Mike Favata • Frank McLaughlin
Mike Micinillio • Tom Brenner
Allan Mogel • Gary A. Lewis

Printed in the United States of America
0 9 8 7 6 5 4 3 2 1

ROAD RUNNER
and
WILE E. COYOTE

in COYOTE CAPERS

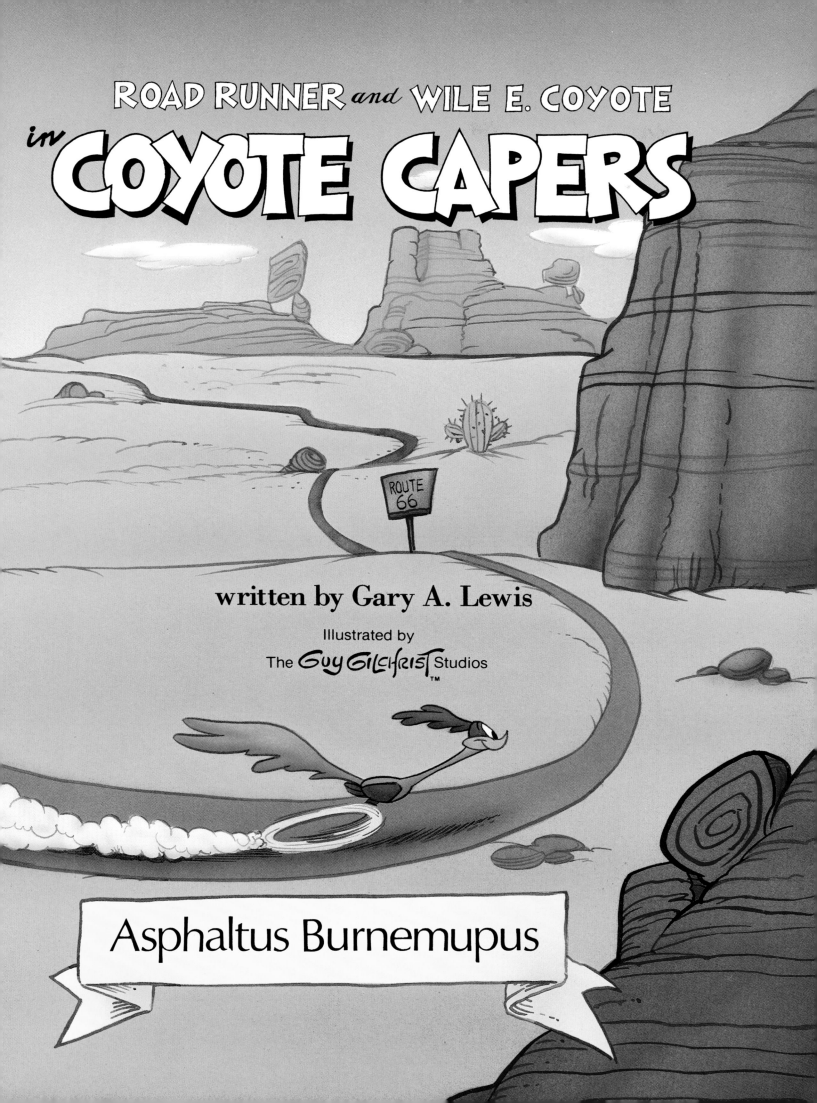

Wile E. Coyote's mother had a favorite saying. It was, "If at first you don't succeed, try, try again."

Wile E. was a good son, and he always listened to what his mother told him. But no matter what Wile E. tried, when it came to catching that pesky Road Runner, nothing seemed to work.

One afternoon, though, Wile E. Coyote saw something in the local papers that made him forget all about Road Runners.

"Acme Pictures is about to make their next movie—a new western," Wile E. read. "The director will be looking for local talent in the next few days." Acme president I. M. Ritch told this reporter, "We're looking for a new face to turn into a big star."

This it it, thought Wile E.—my chance to get out of this dump and become a star! I'll be famous. I'll be rich. I'll knock their socks off!

The Acme Pictures film crew arrived in the mesa bright and early on a Monday morning. Wile E. Coyote was there to meet them. The director took one look at him and ordered a screen test.

It took Wile E. five hours to get dressed for the screen test. When he was finished, he looked perfect.

Wile E. just knew he was going to get the part! Soon, he would be the biggest star Hollywood had ever seen!

First, he impressed everyone with his roping skills.

At least, he intended to impress everyone. Instead, just as he was doing his biggest trick, that pesky Road Runner came zipping by and destroyed his concentration.

"I'd like to go on," he told the director. "But I'm all tied up right now."

Then, he impressed everyone with his riding skills.
At least, he intended to impress everyone. Instead, just as he was doing his biggest trick, that pesky Road Runner came zipping by and destroyed his concentration.

"I'd like to continue," he told the director, "but my pony is a little hoarse."

After that, he impressed everyone with his sharp-shooting skills. At least, he intended to impress everyone. Instead, just as he was doing his biggest trick, that pesky Road Runner came zipping by and destroyed his concentration.

"I'd like to continue," he told the director, "but my feet are killing me."

Next, he stopped a runaway stagecoach. At least, he was going to stop a runaway stagecoach. Instead, just as he was standing there,

that rotten Road Runner came zipping by and destroyed his concentration. "I'd like to continue," he told the director, "but I'm flat broke."

BEEP! BEEP!

"I can even do my own stunts!" he assured the director. "Just watch as I dive off the top of this high building."

Unfortunately, the mattress Wile E. was supposed to land on had a little more bounce than he expected.

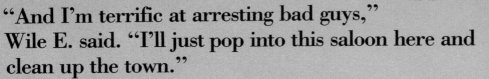

"And I'm terrific at arresting bad guys," Wile E. said. "I'll just pop into this saloon here and clean up the town."

NO DANCING
NO SINGING
NO HAVING FUN
"Have a good time"

Unfortunately, before he could do anything, Wile E. tripped over a strongbox in the middle of the room.

The last thing Wile E. meant to do was to impress everyone with his great romantic qualities.

At least he intended to impress everyone. But the only thing that impressed his costar were some cactus spines.

Even so, Wile E. just knew the director was impressed…
particularly with how well he could take a punch. And that female
coyote could certainly throw a mean one.

And Wile E. was right.
The director *was* impressed.

"That's it!" the director shouted. "I'm impressed! Cut! Cut! We've found our star!"

Wile E. was delighted. *This is it!* he thought. *This is the moment I'm going to become a big star!*

The director was not only impressed—he was delighted. But he was delighted with…the *Road Runner???*

"You're perfect for the part," he told the bird. "And to think you were out here in the mesa all along! I want to sign you to a five-year contract. No, make that a ten-year contract. We'll pay you five million dollars! No, make that ten million!"

THE INSTANT-OVER-NIGHT-SENSATION GET-FAMOUS IN A HURRY CONTRACT

Sign here___

34

"I don't believe it!" shouted Wile E. "If that varmint becomes a famous star, I'll eat my hat!"
And that's exactly what Wile E. did.

For a while after that, things went on as usual. Wile E. tried and tried…and failed and failed.

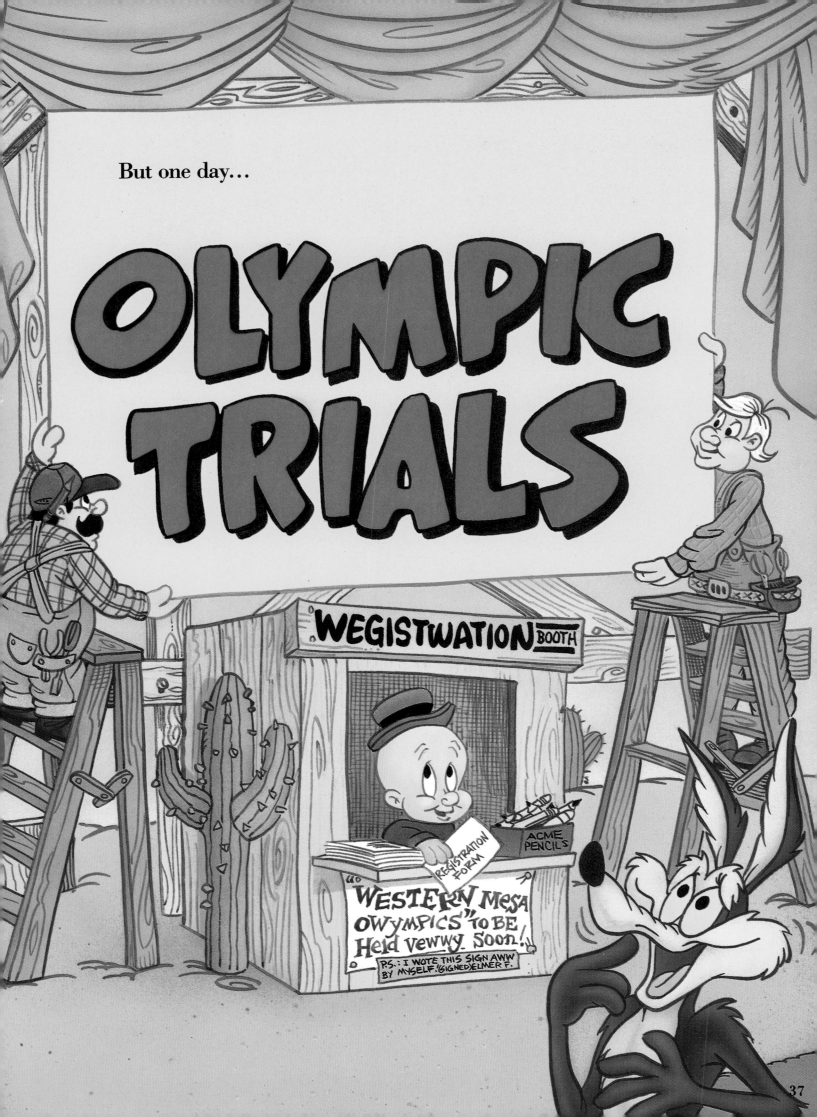

Wile E. Coyote was going to be a star—a star of track and field. The western division tryouts for the Olympics were being held right in the neighborhood, and he was going to win a place on the team!

Wile E. trained for months at Jack LaLion's gym. He did push-ups and sit-ups and lifted barbells. Finally, he was ready.

The day of the tryouts, Wile E. felt fit and strong and ready to compete.

But who was that signing up just ahead of him? It was the Road Runner!

Wile E. was delighted. *This is my chance,* he thought, *to get back at that puny little feather duster. I'll show him what it means to be a great athlete!*

The first event of the day was the swim meet. Wile E. just knew he could win. After all, he could swim rings around that flat-footed Road Runner. Why, Wile E. Coyote could swim the English channel backwards and blindfolded with one paw tied behind his back in the time it took that nuisance of a bird to swim a lap in his bathtub. He could swim the Atlantic Ocean while the Road Runner was saying "Beep!" and the Pacific Ocean in the time it took that bird to say a second "Beep!"

"On your mark...get set..." the referee shouted.

Wile E. got off to a fast start. He hit the water with a huge splash. But unfortunately, as Wile E.'s mother was always pointing out, things don't always work out exactly as planned. Wile E. sank to the bottom of the pool like a stone. The Road Runner zipped across the water and reached the finish line before Wile E. could swim a stroke.

But Wile E. was not going to give up. The pole vault was next—and he was definitely going to win it.

Just in case, he had ordered a little something from Acme Athletic Equipment. It was a pair of super-powered jumping shoes.

With these on my feet, Wile E. thought, *I can't lose!*

First, it was the Road Runner's turn. The spectators cheered as he flew over the bar. He made it look easy.

Just wait until I make my jump, thought Wile E. *It'll be over the moon!*

DOINK! DOINK! DOINK!

Wile E. Coyote stepped up to the line, holding his pole. He took a long run, pushed the end of the pole into the ground, and jumped.

It was quite a jump, all right. No one had ever seen anything quite like it before. No one was sure they'd ever see anything like it again, either. They also weren't sure they'd ever see *Wile E.* again.

Luckily, as Wile E.'s mother always used to say, what goes up, must come down.

Wile E. Coyote was furious. He was going to get that pesky Road Runner if it was the last thing he did.

As his mother always used to say, "He who laughs last laughs best." And Wile E. would have the last laugh, all right.

But first he'd have to make a little phone call to the Acme Home Supplies store. He needed some bricks and some paint. When Wile E. was done, the Road Runner wouldn't know what had hit him.

The final event of the Olympic trials was the five hundred yard dash. Wile E. worked quickly, building a wall out of Acme's best bricks and then painting it. *If I finish in time*, he thought happily, *that yellowbellied sap won't finish at all!*

When he was finished, Wile E. stood back to admire his handiwork. The wall he had built looked just like the end of the track. The Road Runner would hit it at a hundred miles an hour. *And I'll win the race!* Wile E. thought, grinning.

"On your mark…get set…go!
The race had begun, and the Road Runner was already in front by four hundred yards. It looked like he was definitely going to win.
That's what he *thinks*, Wile E. thought.

Wile E. watched gleefully. The Road Runner was nearing the finish line. He was almost at the finish line. Then he *was* at the finish line! The Road Runner was the winner! The crowds cheered. The band played.

Wile E. Coyote couldn't believe his eyes. *What did I do wrong?* he wondered. *How could that heap of pinfeathers run right through a brick wall?*

If that Road Runner can run straight through a brick wall, so can I! Wile E. thought.

But he thought wrong.

How'd he do it? wondered Wile E. *How'd he do it? Oh, my aching head!*

The Road Runner, of course, won the race. But at least Wile E. had a good night's sleep.

And as his mother was always saying, "Sweet dreams!"